Hi guys! Today is going to be totally awesome !!!!

You want to know why?

This book belongs to:

_____

Because today is the day I get to go to my first martial arts lesson!
And I'm super excited and totally pumped!

Say would you like to come along with me?

Library of Congress Control Number: 2020911406

To reach Ocean Aire Productions, Inc. visit: www.AdventuresofHarryandFriends.com

This is a Black Belt Principles Series: Book Two
Created & Written by Sarah Beliza Tucker- Illustrated by Adam Ihle - Edited by Kim Siebels

ISBN Print: 978-1-7334684-2-8
ISBN Digital: 978-1-7334684-3-5

Great! Let's go...

Created & Written by
Sarah Beliza Tucker
Illustrated by Adam Ihle

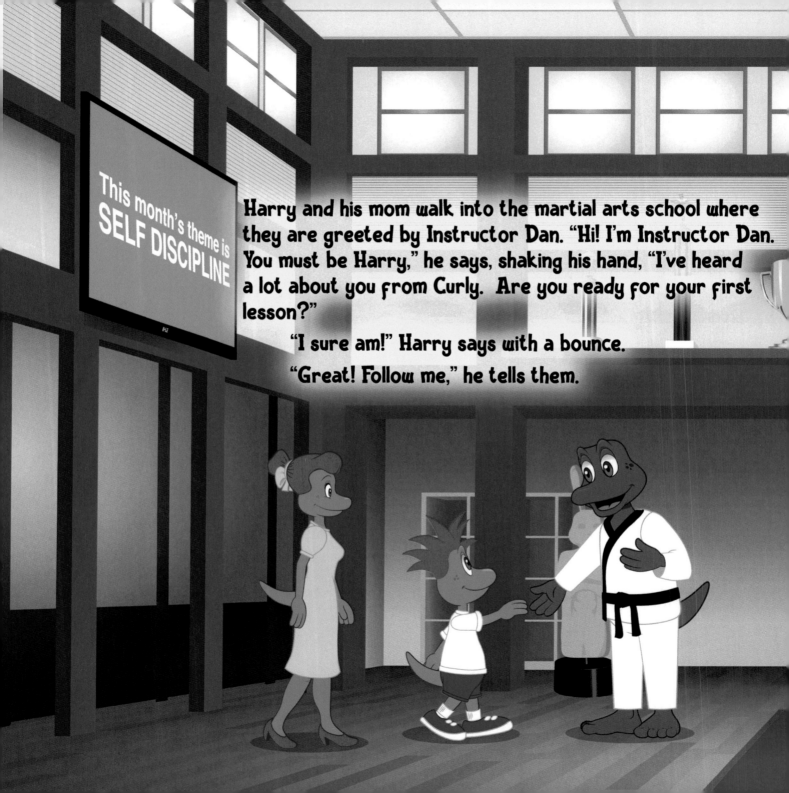

This month's theme is
SELF DISCIPLINE

Harry and his mom walk into the martial arts school where they are greeted by Instructor Dan. "Hi! I'm Instructor Dan. You must be Harry," he says, shaking his hand, "I've heard a lot about you from Curly. Are you ready for your first lesson?"

"I sure am!" Harry says with a bounce.

"Great! Follow me," he tells them.

Instructor Dan guides them through his school to a private room where he teaches Harry...

AIM HIGHER

PERSEVERANCE
MEANS
NEVER GIVE UP

"This is so much fun!" Harry says with a giggle.

"I'm glad you're having fun, but do you know what's even better than all this training?" he asks.

"Nope," Harry replies.

"That's no sir," Instructor Dan tells him.

"Remember, it's important to always answer your teachers and parents with respect, like saying yes and no ma'am, or mom or dad or sir. Do you know why this is so important?" he asks.

"No...sir?" he answers with a question.

Instructor Dan laughs and says, "Because it makes us feel good, and it also tells us you are listening. Now it's time for the most important part of this lesson. Are you ready?"

"Yes, sir!" Harry responds.

"Great!" Instructor Dan says.

Harry and his mom sit quietly and listen to what Instructor Dan says.

This month's theme is SELF DISCIPLINE

A short time later, Harry skips out of the room towards his new friends and says, "Hi guys!"

"How did it go?" Curly asks.

"It was totally awesome! Thank you so much for inviting me," Harry tells him.

"That's great. You're going to love this school," Ricky says.

"Oh, I forgot! Ricky, this is Harry...Harry, this is Ricky. He's testing for his black belt soon," Curly tells him.

"Wow!...

...I can't wait to be a black belt one day!" Harry says excitedly.

"You can do it. It just takes self-discipline and a whole lot of perseverance. Which means we don't give up when things get hard," Ricky explains.

"That's what Instructor Dan, said too!" Harry says, then notices his mom waving at him. "Well, I guess I have to go. See you guys at school tomorrow."

"Oh, not me. My brothers, and sister and I are home-schooled. But I will see you here in class," Ricky tells Harry.

"Home-schooled?" Harry asks curiously.

"It's like going to a private school at home where our parents are our teachers," Ricky answers him.

"That's cool. My mom's a teacher too," Harry says.

"If you want, you should come to my Black Belt Ceremony. It's in about four weeks. We're also going to have a hopping party in the park after the ceremony," Ricky tells him.

"Oh boy! I would love to go!" Harry says.

"Harry," his mom calls out.

"Well, I've got to go.
See you guys later!"
He waves goodbye.

"I can't wait to come back, Mom! Thank you for bringing me," he says.

A few minutes later, Harry bounces into his room. "I'm home!" he announces to his Captain Karate Man doll that is sitting on his bed. "I have so much to tell you!"

"Today, I had my first martial arts lesson where I learned all about the attention stance, which looks like this," Harry says. Then he pauses for a moment. "When I'm at attention, I don't move a muscle, even if a ladybug lands on my nose. I don't move.

Then I learned about courtesy, which is this cool bow.

It's like saying hello and goodbye when I step onto the mat before class and after."

"Oh, I almost forgot, Captain Karate Man. The most important part is my student creed," Harry says.

"Number One says, 'I intend to develop myself in a positive manner and to avoid anything that would reduce my mental growth or my physical health.' "

Harry pauses for a moment and says, "This means that we should eat healthier foods like more fruits and vegetables and less candy. We should also work hard in school so we become smart, too.

Number Two says, 'I intend to develop self-discipline in order to bring out the best in myself and others.'

That means I should show self-discipline, like if I make a mess in my room, I should clean it up without being asked," Harry tells him.

Harry continues, "Now the last one, and this is a little hard, but it says, 'I intend to use what I learn in class con-struc-tively' - he stumbles through the words - 'and de-fen-sive-ly to help myself and my fellow man and never to be abusive or offensive.'

That means we don't ever use what we learn in class to hurt others, no matter how angry they might make us," he says.

"Now isn't that cool?" Harry asks, and looks at Captain Karate Man as if he is talking to him.

Then Harry responds, "You're right, Captain Karate Man, my room is a little messy, and Instructor Dan did say to show self-discipline. I should clean up after myself without my mom or dad telling me to do it."

Harry stops, looks around his room and proudly states, "I must have

SELF - DISCIPLINE.

Mom and Dad are going to be super proud of me!" Then he skips out his bedroom door for dinner.

"Instructor Dan...Instructor Dan!"
Harry says, jumping up and down.

"I know my student creed!" Harry says proudly, and in that moment he rattles off the entire student creed. Then gasps for air.

"Oh...Wow! And all in one breath! Harry, you've just earned your white belt," Instructor Dan says.

The class stops and drums the floor as Harry's first belt is tied around his waist!
"You are now on your way to becoming an amazing black belt one day," then gives
him a high five and says, " but first, let's finish up your second lesson and get you
in class."

"Yippee!"

Harry shouts and jumps for joy.

"This is the best day of my life!" Harry whispers, and gives Instructor Dan a great big hug.

Wow! What an amazing adventure!

I joined the coolest martial arts school in the world!

I've only had two lessons, and I've already learned all about SELF-DISCIPLINE, and RESPECT for myself and others, and we should also try to eat healthier foods.

I also met a new friend! His name is Ricky. He's home-schooled and he's almost a black belt!
He even invited me to his Black Belt Ceremony and party.

You should come too!
It's going to be epic!
I can't wait until I'm a black belt!

How about you?

Just remember, all we need is a little self-discipline, respect and perseverance, which means we don't give up when things get hard. I learned that from Ricky.

Also, if you want a sneak peek at our next adventure, get your parents' permission and go to:

www.AdventuresOfHarryAndFriends.com and join our club.

Well, I have to go!
I hear my Mom
calling me.

See you soon!
Bye for now!